Retold by Anna Claybourne

Illustrated by Tom Morgan-Jones

First published in paperback in 2016

Wayland
An imprint of
Hachette Children's Group
Part of Hodder & Stoughton
Carmelite House
50 Victoria Embankment
London EC4Y 0DZ

Editor: Elizabeth Brent
Design: Amy McSimpson
Illustration: Tom Morgan-Jones

Dewey number: 823.9'2-dc23

10 9 8 7 6 5 4 3 2 1

ISBN: 978 0 7502 8116 4
Library eBook ISBN: 978 0 7502 9367 9

Printed in China
An Hachette UK company
www.hachette.co.uk
www.hachettechildrens.co.uk

CONTENTS

"Well, you're wrong! Ladies love me, apart from you, of course. It's just a shame I'm not one for romance."

"Luckily for the ladies," Beatrice said.

"Gentlemen!" Don Pedro announced over the chatter. "Leonato has kindly invited us to stay with him for a month – or as long as we like."

Much Ado About Nothing: Who's who?

Each Shakespeare play begins with a list of characters, or *dramatis personae*. Here are the characters in *Much Ado*:

Chapter One

Leonato, governor of Messina, was relaxing in his garden when a messenger arrived with a letter. As he read it, Leonato sat up suddenly. “Don Pedro is coming back!” he exclaimed. His daughter, Hero, and her cousin Beatrice looked up from their books.

"So the battle really *is* over?" Leonato asked the messenger.

"Yes, my lord. They scored a great victory!"

"And it says here that Claudio fought particularly bravely." Hearing that name, Hero held her breath.

"That's right, sir. Claudio may look young and innocent, but he fights like a lion."

Beatrice got up, and peered at Leonato's letter. "I suppose Mr Know-It-All is back too?" she asked.

"Mr who?"

"She means Benedick," Leonato sighed.

"Oh, Benedick. Yes, he's back. Another brilliant fighter on the battlefield," said the messenger.

"Oh, is he?" said Beatrice. "If only he were as much use back home!"

"But he is, my lady," said the messenger. "He's polite, witty, and a good friend to Claudio and Don Pedro. Benedick is full of virtues."

"Full of himself, more like," Beatrice mumbled.

"Ignore my niece," said Leonato. "She and Benedick don't get on. They're always arguing."

"Yes, and I always win," added Beatrice.

"Oh, Beatrice," said Leonato. "You're never going to fall for any man, are you?"

"Nope," said Beatrice.

"They're here!" shouted the messenger, as Don Pedro and his men came in, wearing their army uniforms. Hero grabbed Beatrice's arm excitedly.

"Don Pedro!" Leonato cried, hugging him. "Congratulations on the battle! We're all so happy to see you back safe and well."

Don Pedro bowed to Hero, and she blushed. "Your daughter is more beautiful than ever," he told Leonato. "And she looks just like you!"

"Well, hardly," butted in Benedick. "I hope you're not telling her she looks like a middle-aged man!"

Don Pedro laughed. "I don't mean that!" he said.

"I'm amazed you're still cracking jokes, Benedick," said Beatrice. "No one takes any notice of you."

"Oh, it's you," Benedick said. "Lady Scornful."

"I'm sure all ladies are scornful when you're around," Beatrice retorted.

"Well, you're wrong! Ladies love me, apart from you, of course. It's just a shame I'm not one for romance."

"Luckily for the ladies," Beatrice said.

"Gentlemen!" Don Pedro announced over the chatter. "Leonato has kindly invited us to stay with him for a month – or as long as we like."

"You're all welcome here," said Leonato. "You too, Don John," he told Don Pedro's solemn-looking brother. "I know you and Don Pedro haven't always been the best of friends, but that's all in the past now. You're my guest, just as much as he is."

"Thanks," said Don John.

"Let's go in. I'll show you all to your rooms," Leonato said cheerily. They headed indoors, leaving just Benedick and Claudio outside.

"Benedick..." Claudio began. "Did you see Hero, Leonato's daughter?"

"Of course. What about her?"

"Oh Benedick – she's even more beautiful than when I last saw her! And she's so sweet and shy and lovely! Don't you agree?"

"I suppose she's all right," said Benedick. "But Claudio, don't tell me you're in love!"

"Sorry, Benedick," Claudio sighed. "I'd marry Hero tomorrow, if she'd have me."

What does that mean!?

Benedick says he doesn't love anyone, and Beatrice says that's a "dear happiness", meaning a precious bit of good luck, for women.

Don Pedro came back out. “Come on, guys. Come inside. What are you talking about?”

“Claudio is in love,” Benedick sighed. “With Hero.”

“It’s true.” Claudio blushed.

“Well, that’s a good thing!” said Don Pedro. “You’d be perfect for each other.”

“A *good* thing!?” said Benedick incredulously. “To fall in love and tie yourself to a woman, like an ox pulling a plough? That’s something I’ll never do.”

“You’ll change your mind.” Don Pedro smiled.

“I will not.” Benedick scowled.

“Really... perfect for each other?” Claudio was saying. “Don Pedro – I adore her, but I don’t even know where to start. Whenever I go near her, I’m tongue-tied.”

“Then I’ll help,” said Don Pedro. “Leonato is throwing a party tonight. It's fancy dress. I’ll talk to Hero, and make sure she knows how you feel. If she likes you too, I’ll ask Leonato if he’d agree to you marrying her.”

I shall see thee, ere I die, look pale with love.
With anger, with sickness, or with hunger, my lord, not with love.
What does that mean!?
"Thee" means you and "ere" means before.

Later, Leonato was talking to his brother Antonio about the music for the celebrations.

"It's all under control," said Antonio. "But Leonato... my servant was in the garden just now, and he thought he heard Don Pedro saying he was going to tell Hero that he loves her! Tonight, at the party!"

"Really?" gasped Leonato. "Don Pedro?" This was a surprise. "Well, we must tell my daughter, so that she can think about how she wants to reply."

Upstairs, Don John and his servant Conrad were talking.

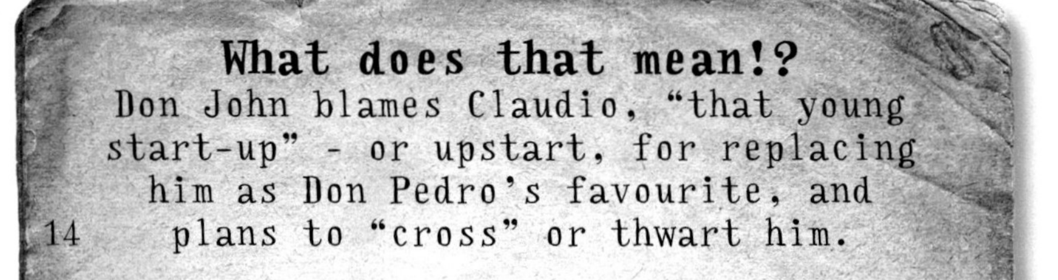

"What's wrong, sir?" asked Conrad. "You seem unhappy."

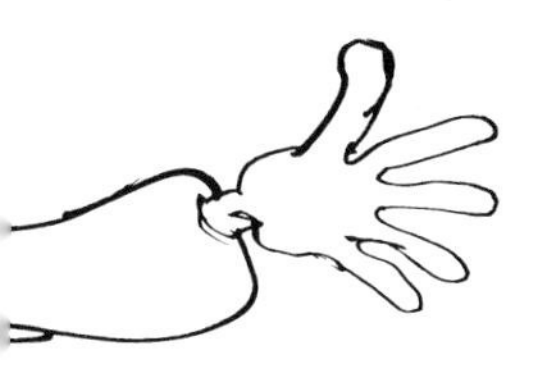

"I don't smile for no reason," said Don John. "That's just who I am. Oh, Don Pedro and I are friends again, that's what everyone thinks. But I've seen how he looks at me. He still thinks I'm scum. He'd still rather hang out with his golden boy Claudio, than with his own brother."

Then Don John's other servant Borachio came in. "Sir, I've just overheard your brother and Claudio talking. Claudio is in love with Hero, and Don Pedro is going to help him to win her hand in marriage."

"Ugh! Perfect, precious little Claudio," Don John sneered. "My brother will do anything for him, but I get nothing. If I can find a way to ruin this love match, well..." He smirked. "It might be just the thing to cheer me up. Will you help me, boys?"

"At your service." Conrad grinned.

Chapter Two

The ball was about to begin. “Has anyone seen Don John?” Leonato asked. “He seems to have disappeared.”

“Well, not to worry,” said Beatrice. “Who wants to look at his miserable face?”

“He is a bit of a grump,” Hero agreed.

"Now if only a man could be halfway between Don John and Benedick," said Beatrice. "Not too sulky, but not too chatty either. He'd be perfect."

"You'll never find a husband if you're so fussy!" Leonato laughed.

"Then it's lucky I don't want one!" she answered.

"But surely Hero doesn't feel the same," said Antonio. "Your father would like you to get married, Hero. I hope you'll follow his wishes."

"When it comes to husbands, I hope you'll follow your *own* wishes," Beatrice reminded her.

"Of course," said Leonato. "But remember, Hero, Don Pedro is planning to declare his love for you tonight. You must consider your answer carefully."

Before Hero could reply, the soldiers arrived, all wearing party masks. As everyone moved into the ballroom and the music began, Don Pedro approached Hero, and asked her to be his partner.

Hero danced with him politely, but she didn't really want Don Pedro to be in love with her. She wished it was Claudio instead.

Meanwhile, Leonato's servant Balthasar asked Margaret, Hero's lady-in-waiting, to dance. But she rejected him. She already had a much more exciting boyfriend – Don John's servant Borachio.

Why, he is the Prince's jester, a very dull fool.

What does that mean!?

Beatrice describes Benedick as a jester or clown.

As for Beatrice, she danced with Benedick. He had asked her, thinking she couldn't guess who he was. But she could have spotted him a mile away!

"You can't fool me, Benedick," she teased.

"I've never even heard of Benedick," he replied. "Who's he?"

"Oh, he's just Don Pedro's friend – a joker and a fool. He's a terrible dancer, too. In fact, I'm glad you're not him, as he'd probably tread on my feet!"

Benedick was offended, but he kept dancing.

In another part of the ballroom, Don John and Borachio spotted Claudio. Making sure he could hear, they began talking about how Don Pedro was in love with Hero, and had been flirting and dancing with her all evening.

"I heard him say he wants to marry her himself," said Borachio.

"Well, Leonato will be delighted!" said Don John. Then they wandered off, leaving Claudio shocked and heartbroken.

"How could I have been so stupid?" he groaned. "Of course Don Pedro wants Hero for himself! And I can't possibly compete with him!"

Benedick came along. "What's wrong, Claudio?" he said. "Cheer up – it's going brilliantly! Don Pedro's doing a great job!"

"So I've heard," Claudio fumed, and stormed off.

Then Don Pedro appeared too. "What happened?"

"He thinks you've stolen his lady," said Benedick.

"Nonsense – I've done as I promised and told Hero that Claudio loves her," protested Don Pedro. "She's thrilled – and so is her father! Well, Claudio will find out soon enough. But Benedick, look out for Beatrice – she's still being rude about you."

"Oh, for goodness' sake!" Benedick ranted. "Not even a block of wood could put up with so many insults! Do you know, she just said I was a joker and a fool. A fool! Me!"

"Look, here she comes," said Don Pedro.

"Then I'm leaving," said Benedick, walking out.

Beatrice came in with Claudio, who looked sick with jealousy.

"Claudio, don't worry!" Don Pedro said. "Hero knows you love her, and she feels the same! I've told Leonato, and he agrees to the marriage!"

"What?" Claudio gasped. He turned round and saw that Leonato and Hero had come in too. He felt his heart turn upside down and his knees go weak.

“Claudio, I couldn’t wish for a better husband for my daughter – and nor could she,” said Leonato. Claudio stepped forward and took Hero’s hands, staring into her eyes and trembling.

“I–I can’t... I can’t possibly say how happy I am!” Claudio stammered. “Hero, if you will be mine, I will be yours – for ever!”

“Awwww,” said Beatrice, as Leonato shook hands with Claudio. “Well, that’s another couple paired off. Soon I’ll be the only one left on the shelf.”

"I'll find you a husband, Beatrice," said Don Pedro kindly. "I'll even be your husband, if you like."

"No!" exclaimed Beatrice. Then, seeing Don Pedro's shocked face, she quickly added, "I mean, you know I don't want a husband. And I'd be no match for a great, successful man like you."

Beatrice blushed and hurried away, and Don Pedro watched her go. Why had she reacted so strongly? It was almost as if she really loved someone else – but would never admit it.

What does that mean!?

Claudio says his silence is the clearest indication of his happiness. If he were only slightly happy, he could express it, but he is too happy for words.

"She's quite fiery, my niece," said Leonato. "I hope she hasn't hurt your feelings."

"No, no," said Don Pedro. "But I do think it's funny that she's so set against finding a husband."

"Oh, she won't hear of it," agreed Leonato.

"Just like Benedick," said Don Pedro. "In fact, in some ways, they'd be a perfect match!"

"Ha!" snorted Leonato. "If those two were married, they'd drive each other crazy in a week!"

"No, seriously," said Don Pedro, thinking to himself. "When is Claudio and Hero's wedding?"

“It’s planned for Monday,” said Leonato.

“Perfect. By the time the wedding comes around, I bet we can make Beatrice and Benedick fall in love with each other.”

“I’m in!” said Leonato.

“And me,” said Claudio.

“Me too!” said Hero, as she longed for Beatrice to fall in love, like her.

"Then listen," Don Pedro said. "I have a plan."

"Curse it," snarled Don John to Borachio. "I tried to mess things up, but it hasn't worked. Claudio and Hero are engaged, and he's happier than ever."

"I can still think of a way to ruin it all, my lord," smirked Borachio.

"You can? How!?"

"Well," said Borachio, "you know I've been seeing Margaret, who is Hero's lady-in-waiting."

"Yes?"

"All you need to do is tell Claudio and Don Pedro that arranging this marriage was a terrible mistake, because Hero is cheating on Claudio! Tell them you've seen Hero at her bedroom window with her arms around me, Borachio!"

"They'll never believe that," said Don John.

"Then say you'll take them to see it for themselves, the night before the wedding. Bring them to the garden outside Hero's room. But I'll arrange for Margaret to be there, not Hero. You'll see Margaret letting me in through the window, and putting her arms around me, but I'll call her Hero, and they will think it's her."

"Borachio, that is BRILLIANT! Do this for me, and do it well, and a thousand ducats will be yours."

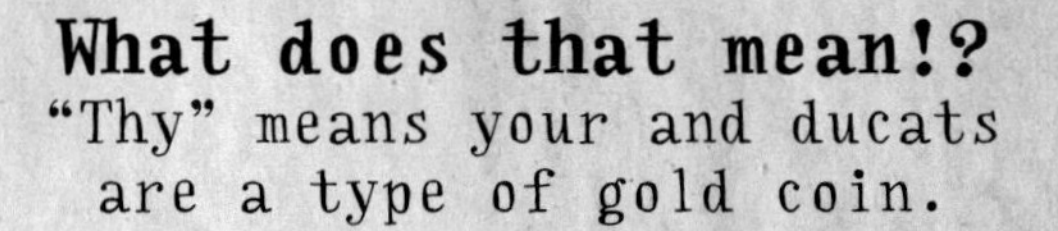
What does that mean!?

"Thy" means your and ducats are a type of gold coin.

Be cunning in the working this,
and thy fee is a thousand ducats.

Benedick lay under a tree in the orchard, moping.

"I thought Claudio was like me," he complained. "We both used to laugh at men who fell in love. And now look at him – he's gone completely soft. Could that happen to me? I don't think so. If it did, the woman would have to be amazing. She'd have to be perfect in every way. She'd have to be—"

Just then he heard Don Pedro and Claudio talking. They were coming into the orchard! Benedick couldn't stand any more soppy love-talk, so he hid behind a bush.

Leonato was with them too, and his servant Balthasar, with his lute.

"What a lovely evening," said Claudio loudly.

"Yes, isn't it? Balthasar, play us a song," said Don Pedro. As Balthasar strummed the lute, Don Pedro whispered, "Did you see where he went?"

"Yes, right behind that bush!" sniggered Claudio.

To the gentle, pretty tune, Balthasar sang:

Ladies, ladies, cry no more –
Men aren't worth your tears.
Ladies, ladies, sigh no more –
It falls upon deaf ears.

Men will always cheat on you,
Ignore you and forget you.
You see, that's just what men are like –
So don't let it upset you!

As the song ended, Don Pedro began talking loudly. "So, Claudio, can it be true? Beatrice is in love with Benedick?"

"Yes, that's what Hero says! Isn't it odd? I never thought she'd fall for any man!" said Claudio.

"Nor did I,"

Leonato joined in. "And least of all Benedick! But she's head over heels, I've heard!"

Behind the hedge, Benedick could hardly believe his ears. Then he began to feel a bit flattered.

What does that mean!?
"Hither" means here and "Signor" means Mr.

"Poor Beatrice," said Claudio. "According to Hero, she writes him love letters, but she can't bear to send them. She knows he'd just laugh at her."

"He would, too," said Don Pedro.

"Yes," said Claudio. "Beatrice is a wonderful woman – beautiful, classy, smart – but Benedick would never see how lucky he was to have her."

"It's a shame, because he's a good catch too," said Don Pedro. "Clever, brave, good-looking..."

"Then maybe we should tell him?" said Leonato.

"No, no, let's not," said Claudio. "I'm sure Beatrice will get over it eventually."

"You're right. Let's go in to dinner," said Leonato.

Benedick was left alone, reeling in amazement.

"She... loves me?" he puzzled. "They sounded as if they really meant it! And they think I would tease her, and not return her love? Do people really think I would do that? Now I think about it, it's true – she is beautiful. She's clever. And she loves me! I don't want to be a proud, sneering fool and hurt her feelings! Oh Beatrice – I'll prove them wrong!"

Chapter Three

The next day, Hero played the exact same trick on Beatrice, with the help of her maidservants, Margaret and Ursula. She told Margaret to go and find Beatrice. "Tell her you've heard me and Ursula talking about her in the garden. With any luck, she'll come and listen!"

Margaret ran off, and a few minutes later, Hero and Ursula saw Beatrice sneaking up behind them, and hiding behind some honeysuckles.

"Perfect!" whispered Hero. Then, more loudly, she said, "No, Ursula, we can't possibly tell Beatrice. She's too scornful. She'd tease him mercilessly."

"But are you really sure he's in love with her?"

"Yes, Claudio and Don Pedro told me! They think I should tell her, but I just can't. It would be better for poor Benedick to suffer in silence."

They were talking about Benedick!? Beatrice couldn't believe it. She leaned a little closer.

"But doesn't Benedick deserve happiness in love, like any other man?"

"Of course, but he wouldn't get that from Beatrice, would he? He may be kind, handsome and brave, but Beatrice can't see that. She'll just find fault and make rude remarks."

"Maybe you're right." Ursula sighed. "But surely even Beatrice would realise how lucky she would be to have him as a husband?"

"No," declared Hero, "we won't tell her. Anyway, come inside, Ursula – I need you and Margaret to help me get my wedding dress ready!"

Sitting alone behind the honeysuckles, Beatrice blushed with shame. "Do people really think that about me?" she wondered. "Maybe it's time to change my ways, and be kinder to poor Benedick. He can't help it if he loves me, after all. So if it's really true, I'll try to love him back."

What does that mean!?

Seeing that she has been judged (condemned) harshly, Beatrice decides to say goodbye - farewell and adieu - to her "maiden" (youthful) scornfulness.

Inside the house, Don Pedro was talking to Claudio, Benedick and Leonato.

"When I go back to Aragon," Don Pedro said, "Claudio should stay here, as it's important for newlyweds to spend time together. Benedick can come with me, of course. There's no danger of you getting married, Benedick, as we know."

"Erm..." began Benedick. "Actually, I've been thinking..."

"What!?" teased Claudio. "What is it, Benedick? Are you in love? At last?"

"Don't be silly," said Don Pedro. "Our Benedick is never falling in love. He's said so quite clearly."

"But he does seem a bit serious," Leonato said.

"I have toothache," said Benedick sheepishly.

"So, toothache makes you wear your smartest clothes, does it?" asked Claudio.

“And is that perfume I smell?” asked Don Pedro.

“He’s in love! I’m sure of it!” Claudio grinned.

“Arrggh, leave me alone!” Benedick huffed. “I need to talk to Leonato in private.”

“I bet he’s going to ask Leonato about marrying Beatrice!” Don Pedro whispered as they left. Just then, Don John came in, his face as stormy as ever.

“I have news,” said Don John. “Bad news, I’m afraid. Claudio, do you plan to marry Hero?”

“Of course he does,” said Don Pedro.

“It’s a bad idea,” said Don John. “You shouldn’t have agreed to it, and you, Don Pedro, should not have helped him. Hero is cheating on Claudio.”

“Hero? I–I don’t believe you!” spluttered Claudio.

“Then come with me, and I’ll show you,” said Don John. “I’ve seen Borachio climb up to her bedroom window, and she lets him in. Every night.”

“It’s not true,” Claudio said, trembling.

“Surely it can’t be!” said Don Pedro.

“Follow me,” said Don John.

What does that mean!?

"I pray you" means I beg you, and "coil" means hustle and bustle.

As dusk fell, Dogberry, Messina's police chief, and his deputy, Verges, stationed a team of guards outside Leonato's house.

"Now, tonight is a special night," Dogberry told them. "It's the night before Leonato's daughter's wedding, and I'm trusting you to keep an eye on his house. George Seacole, you're in charge!"

"Yes, sir!" said Seacole. "What if we see a thief, sir?"

"Oh, stay away from thieves, Seacole. Nasty, low-down people. Don't associate with them!"

"Very good, sir."

"And no chatting and joking on the streets."

"Right you are, sir! Can we go to sleep instead?"

"Of course! But if anything serious happens, come and tell me at once. Goodnight, boys!"

For a few minutes, everything was quiet. Then the policemen saw someone coming along the street, and moved back into the shadows to watch. It was Conrad, Don John's servant, and running up behind him was Borachio.

"Hey, Conrad! It's me! Guess what? I've just earned a thousand ducats from Don John!"

"What? How did you do that!?" asked Conrad.

"I know that man," whispered one of the guards. "He's upto no good."

"Shhh. Did you hear something?" asked Borachio.

"No, nothing. Tell me what you did!" Conrad urged. He was very jealous.

"Well, it was a plan I thought up with Don John. He told Claudio and Don Pedro that Hero was a cheat, and took them to watch outside Hero's bedroom window. Then I came to meet Margaret there, and she let me in – but I called her "Hero". It was dark, and Claudio and Don John thought it really was Hero! Claudio says he's going to the church tomorrow, then at the altar, he'll tell Hero she's a cheat, and call the wedding off!"

The policemen heard every word, staring at each other.

"STOP! POLICE!"

yelled George Seacole. They chased Borachio and Conrad, grabbed them and hauled them back to the police station.

The next morning, Hero's ladies-in-waiting helped her to get dressed. "Oh, madam," sighed Margaret. "You look beautiful! That dress is amazing!"

"But I can't help feeling worried," said Hero. "I don't know why."

"Good morning, Hero," Beatrice said when she came in. "You look nice!"

Hero stared at her, and smiled. "Is that all you have to say, Beatrice? No clever jokes, or moaning about people getting married?"

"Erm... I'm not feeling very well," Beatrice said.

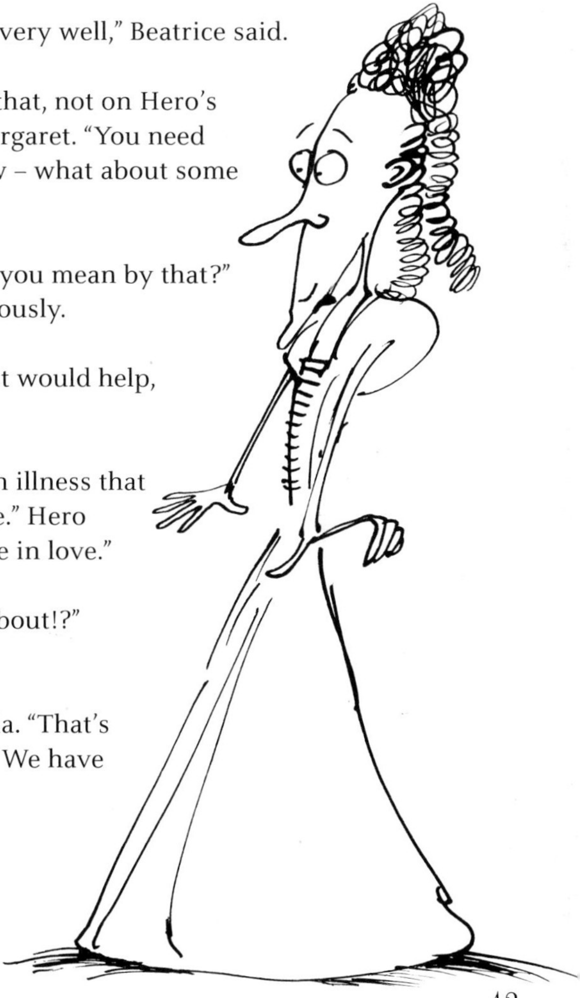

"Oh no, we can't have that, not on Hero's wedding day!" said Margaret. "You need some medicine! I know – what about some Benedictus herb?"

"Benedictus? What do you mean by that?" asked Beatrice, suspiciously.

"Nothing! I just think it would help, that's all."

"Or maybe you have an illness that can't be cured, Beatrice." Hero grinned. "Maybe you're in love."

"What are you all on about!?" snapped Beatrice.

"Oh, listen!" said Ursula. "That's Leonato calling for us. We have to go to the church!"

Leonato stood outside the church in his best clothes, brimming with pride. He greeted all the guests and showed them in. But just as everyone had sat down and the service was about to begin, Dogberry and Verges appeared, shouting, "Sir! Sir!"

"What is it?" he said. "Come on, be quick! Can't you see I'm busy?"

"We'll be quick, sir," said Dogberry.

"Well? Get on with it!"

"We've captured two criminals, sir," said Dogberry.

"Two of the worst criminals you'll ever meet!" added Verges.

"OK, well done. That's your job, isn't it?"

"Sir, we think you should see these men now, and hear what has happened."

"Now!? The wedding's about to start! Everyone's waiting for me!"

"It's very important, sir!"

"Then keep them prisoner, and I'll come later. I don't have time now!"

"Very well, sir," said Dogberry. Leonato rolled his eyes and went into the church.

Chapter Four

"Hero, do you take Claudio to be your husband?" asked the Friar.

"I do," said Hero, bursting with happiness.

"And Claudio, do you take Hero to be your wife?"

Claudio did not smile. "No," he said.

The Friar looked puzzled. "Is there any reason why you should not be married?" he asked.

"Is there a reason, Hero?" Claudio asked coldly.

"No, none at all!" said Hero, looking upset.

"Leonato," Claudio said. "Do you give me Hero as my wife?"

"Yes, of course," said Leonato.

"Then have her back!" shouted Claudio. "How could you give your friend something so worthless and horrible?"

Hero gasped at him in shock.

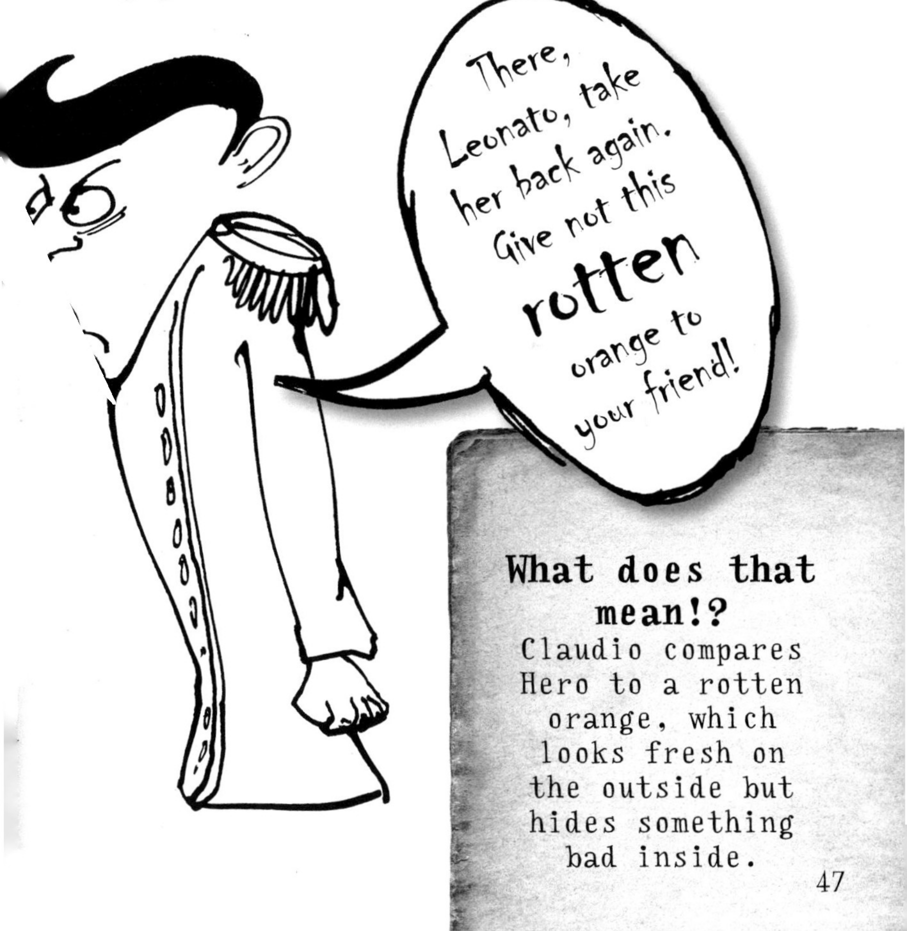

What does that mean!?

Claudio compares Hero to a rotten orange, which looks fresh on the outside but hides something bad inside.

“She looks so innocent, doesn’t she? But she’s not!” Claudio ranted. “I know what she really is – a cheat who lets other men into her room at night!”

“What are you talking about!?” Hero demanded.

“Tell me, Hero,” said Claudio accusingly. “Who was that man you kissed and hugged, and let in through your bedroom window last night?”

“I didn’t see any man last night!” protested Hero.

“I’m sorry, Leonato. Claudio is right,” said Don Pedro. “I was with him and Don John last night when we saw them. Hero has another boyfriend.”

“Hero, how could you do this?” Leonato asked.

Overcome with shock, Hero fainted, and Beatrice and Benedick both rushed forward to help her.

“Let’s leave this sorry scene,” said Don John. He walked out of the church with Claudio and Don Pedro. Slowly, everyone else got up and left too.

Beatrice tried to wake Hero, but she couldn’t. “Oh my lady,” she wept. “My cousin... she’s dead!”

But then Hero moved, and opened her eyes. The Friar knelt down and spoke to her gently. “Don’t worry, Hero my dear. You’ve had a shock, but we’ll sort this out.”

“Sort this out!?” Leonato roared. “After what she did? Don Pedro and Claudio wouldn’t lie!”

"Listen, sir," said the Friar. "I was right next to her, and I saw her face. I've never seen someone look so shocked and upset. I'm sure she's innocent. And I have an idea. Tell everyone Hero is dead, and hide her away. Meanwhile, we can find out the truth."

Leonato didn't know what else to do, so he agreed, and helped the Friar to take Hero to a hiding place. Benedick and Beatrice were left alone.

"Beatrice, don't cry," Benedick said. "I believe Hero is innocent."

"I wish some man would take revenge for her, then!" Beatrice sobbed.

"Can I do anything?"

"There is something, but you'd never do it."

"Try me," said Benedick. "I'll do whatever you ask. I love you, Beatrice. I know that sounds strange."

"I was about to say the same thing, but you got in first," Beatrice sniffed.

"Go on, then – say it."

Beatrice gulped. "I... I love you, Benedick!"

Benedick took her hand. "Now, tell me what I can do for you – ask me anything."

Beatrice wiped her eyes with her hands. "Kill Claudio," she said.

Benedick was shocked. "No! I can't kill my friend!"

"Then you don't love me," said Beatrice, bursting into tears again. "Claudio has broken poor, sweet Hero's heart, and she's done nothing wrong! How dare he accuse her like that! How dare he! Oh, if only I was a man, I would rip him to pieces!"

"Beatrice, please," said Benedick. "I can't just kill him. But I can challenge him to a duel for what he's done. That's what I'll do. Now, go and look after Hero – I must spread the word that she has died."

As Leonato was still busy, Dogberry and Verges went to see the town clerk, who wrote down records of all the crimes, weddings and other events that took place in Messina. They took Borachio and Conrad with them, along with the policemen.

In front of the town clerk, the policemen repeated everything they had heard Borachio say – including the fact that Don John had agreed to the trick, and had paid Borachio a thousand ducats.

"It's all lies," protested Borachio, tugging at his handcuffs. "I never did any of that!"

"We're innocent men!" Conrad wailed.

"Then why," said the town clerk, "did Claudio accuse Hero of exactly what you have described, this very morning, when they were supposed to be getting married? The poor girl fainted and died there and then from the shock! And perhaps you can also explain why Don John has disappeared – run away from Messina before dawn?"

Borachio and Conrad hung their heads.

"Let's take these men to Leonato at once," said the town clerk, "so he can hear the truth for himself."

Chapter Five

Leonato was pacing to and fro when Claudio and Don Pedro passed by.

"Claudio!" Leonato said. "If you have wrongly accused Hero, I'll make you pay in a fight to the death. Your words broke her heart, and killed her."

Claudio felt terrible. "Sir, I'm sorry about Hero, but I can't fight you. I couldn't do that to you."

"Claudio has done no wrong," said Don Pedro. "He saw what she did with his own eyes."

Leonato couldn't stand it any more, so he stormed out. Then Benedick came in.

"Benedick!" Don Pedro said. "Maybe you can cheer us up!"

But Benedick wasn't smiling. "Claudio, I challenge you to a duel," he said. "Your false words killed Hero, and I'm here to defend her good name. And no, I'm not joking."

"OK," said Claudio. "I'm not scared of you."

"And Don Pedro," Benedick went on, "you should know your brother Don John has fled Messina."

"Leonato! Where is Leonato?" It was Dogberry and his troupe of policemen, dragging Borachio and Conrad in chains.

"What's going on!?" Don Pedro asked.

Staring sadly at his feet, Borachio told Don Pedro the whole story. "It was my idea," he confessed, "but Don John wanted me to do it, to ruin the wedding. He paid me well." He began to sob. "I never thought poor Hero would end up dead."

Claudio had turned white. "Oh, Hero... I'm so sorry," he whispered.

Leonato and Antonio came in with the town clerk, who had told them the news. "Is this the man?" Leonato demanded.

"Yes, sir. It was me," mumbled Borachio.

"But you two played a part as well, didn't you?" said Leonato, turning to Claudio and Don Pedro.

"Leonato, I know you can't forgive me," Claudio said. "But take your revenge on me however you see fit. I'll do whatever you say."

"The same for me," said Don Pedro.

"Well, you can't give me my daughter back," said Leonato. "But I want you both to tell everyone in Messina the truth about her – that she was innocent and faithful. Claudio, write a poem about her, to put on her gravestone. And there's one more thing."

"Anything," said Claudio.

"My brother Antonio has a daughter," said Leonato. "Now Hero is dead, she's the only child we have between us. You will make amends, Claudio, by marrying her, and the wedding will be tomorrow. Do that for me, and I will forgive you."

Claudio had begun to cry. "Thank you sir, for your kindness," he sniffed. "I will do as you ask."

"All right then," said Leonato. "We're done here. I will see you at the church tomorrow."

What does that mean!?

"Doth" means does. Claudio says Leonato's leniency moves him to tears.

Benedick was trying to write Beatrice a love letter, but he was hopeless at it. When he saw her coming, he quickly stuffed it into his pocket.

"So," said Beatrice. "Did you challenge Claudio?"

"Yes, I did," said Benedick. "So he'll have to fight me, or else be called a coward. Beatrice..."

"What?"

"What is it about me that you love?"

"Oh, I don't know." Beatrice blushed. "You have so many terrible qualities, they all kind of roll into one. What about *you*? Why do you love *me*?"

"I can't imagine," said Benedick. "I didn't mean it to happen – it's just something I have to suffer!"

Then Ursula ran in. "Come quickly!" she panted. "You'll never guess what's happened! Hero is innocent! It was all a trick! It was Don John's doing – and he's run away!"

The next morning, at dawn, Claudio and Don Pedro stood in the graveyard. Claudio hung a poem on the grave that Leonato had put there.

Here lies Hero, killed by evil lies,
Told by mistaken fools who did her wrong.
Although that lovely lady lives no more,
Her good name lives for ever in this song.

"Goodbye, Hero," Claudio said sadly.

"Come on, Claudio," said Don Pedro. "We have to go to your wedding."

Leonato was waiting at the church, along with Antonio, Benedick and Beatrice, the Friar, and Hero and her ladies-in-waiting. They covered Hero's face with a veil as Claudio and Don Pedro came into the church.

"This way," said Leonato, taking Claudio up to the front. "Here comes the one you are to marry." Antonio led Hero up the aisle.

"My lady, can I see your face?" asked Claudio.

"Once you're married," said Leonato. The Friar asked them if they took each other as husband and wife, and they both said they did.

"I'll be as good a husband to you as any man ever could," Claudio promised.

"Let's hope so," said Hero, lifting up her veil. Claudio's mouth dropped open. "Hero?"

"Hero? But Hero died!" Don Pedro gasped.

"Yes," Hero said. "One Hero did die – that cruel, cheating Hero created by rumours, who never really existed. But I'm still here."

Claudio kissed Hero and held her in his arms, saying sorry over and over again.

What does that mean!?

Hero says that the "defiled" or wrongly accused Hero has died.

"Erm – Friar..." It was Benedick. "Before we leave the church, I have something to ask Beatrice. Beatrice... do you love me?" Beatrice couldn't bear to admit it in front of all her friends. "No! What are you talking about?"

"Oh!" said Benedick. "Then Leonato, Don Pedro and Claudio must be mistaken. They said you did!"

"Why?" said Beatrice. "Do you love me?"

"No! Not at all!" protested Benedick.

"But Hero and Ursula said you did!"

"Whatever. So you don't love me then?"

"Nope." Beatrice shrugged. "Not really!"

"Come on, Beatrice," said Leonato. "I think you do love Benedick."

"And I know he loves you," said Claudio, "because look – I found this letter in one of his pockets!" He threw it to Beatrice.

"And we found this one," said Hero. "It was in Beatrice's room." She handed it to Benedick.

"Well, isn't that amazing," said Benedick, as they read each other's embarrassing love notes. "OK, Beatrice – I'll marry you. But only out of pity."

"How dare you!" Beatrice shouted. "I'll marry you, but only to save you from dying of a broken heart!

"For goodness' sake," said Benedick. "I know how to stop you arguing." He went over to her, took her in his arms and kissed her, and she threw her arms around his neck, as everyone clapped and cheered.

The Friar agreed to perform a second wedding on the spot, and Antonio struck up the wedding band. And as they all danced, a messenger came in with news for Don Pedro.

"Your brother Don John has been caught," he said. "He's in prison here in Messina, waiting for you and Leonato to decide what to do with him."

"Forget about him until tomorrow," said Benedick, taking Don Pedro's hand. "Come and dance!"

What does that mean!?

Benedick says he'll stop Beatrice from talking by kissing her.

MUCH ADO ABOUT NOTHING AT A GLANCE

Much Ado About Nothing is about two couples, and the very different obstacles that stand in their way. While Don John's evil plot threatens the pure, young love of Claudio and Hero, the older Beatrice and Benedick are their own worst enemies, refusing to admit their love for each other.

War of words

Although Claudio and Hero's story forms the main plot, Benedick and Beatrice have much more to say. Thanks to their witty banter, passionate arguments and awkward love scenes, they are among Shakespeare's most vivid and lifelike characters.

Plays and dialogue

This book retells *Much Ado* in prose, but Shakespeare wrote it as a play to be performed by actors. It has no descriptions or narrative, just lines of dialogue, or speech, and a few stage directions. Here you can see a scene from *Much Ado About Nothing*, as Shakespeare wrote it:

ACT 2

Scene I. [A hall in Leonato's house]
Enter Leonato, Antonio his brother, Hero his daughter, and Beatrice his niece. ← Stage directions

LEONATO: Was not Count John here at supper?
ANTONIO: I saw him not.
BEATRICE: How tartly that gentleman looks. I can never see him but I am heartburned an hour after.

FACT FILE:

FULL TITLE: *Much Ado About Nothing*

DATE WRITTEN: Probably 1598

LENGTH: 2,581 lines

Acts and scenes

Like Shakespeare's other plays, *Much Ado* is divided into five main sections or acts, and smaller scenes. Each scene has its own setting, usually somewhere in Leonato's house or garden. The acts and scenes give the play its structure, and break it up into short, easy chunks for actors to learn.

THE FIVE ACTS OF *MUCH ADO*

ACT 1 (3 scenes)

Don Pedro's men visit Leonato, Beatrice and Benedick bicker, while Claudio falls in love with Hero.

ACT 2 (3 scenes)

Don John plans to destroy Claudio and Hero's happiness. The others hatch a plot to set up Benedick and Beatrice.

ACT 3 (5 scenes)

Don John's servant Borachio tricks Claudio into thinking Hero is cheating on him, while Benedick and Beatrice's friends trick them both into thinking the other loves them.

ACT 4 (2 scenes)

At the wedding, Claudio rejects Hero. Benedick shows his love for Beatrice by taking Hero's side against Claudio.

ACT 5 (4 scenes)

Don John's plot is revealed, and Benedick and Beatrice are forced to declare their love. At last, both couples can marry.

THE STORY OF *MUCH ADO ABOUT NOTHING*

Though Shakespeare is famous for the exciting, emotional and lifelike stories he told, he didn't actually make them all up himself. He borrowed most of his plots from old stories, myths, legends or history books, sometimes combining them or changing the details to create something new.

Mixed-up lovers

For *Much Ado*, Shakespeare was probably inspired by several stories told and retold by Italian and French writers of the late 1500s, such as Ludovico Ariosto and François de Belleforest. Their works often featured the theme of a happy couple being tricked into suspecting each other of cheating. Ariosto's *Orlando Furioso* probably gave Shakespeare the story of Claudio, Hero and Don John, though he made up new names for them.

Sparring partners

Shakespeare may also have used *The Book of the Courtier* by Italian writer Baldassare Castiglione, which discusses ideas of gentlemanly behaviour. It includes a character called Pallavicino who declares how unimpressed he is with women, but is forced to change his mind. He often argues with a female character – Emilia Pia. They could have been the inspiration for Beatrice and Benedick.

Where was Messina?

Unlike some other Shakespeare plays, there's no evidence that anyone in *Much Ado About Nothing* was ever a real person. However, the setting of the play, Messina, was and still is a real place. It is a port in Sicily – an island that is now part of Italy.

The battles that provide a background to the play were based on the real, historical Italian Wars of the early 1500s. For some of that time, the city of Messina was under the control of Aragon in Spain, and Don Pedro in the play comes from Aragon.

SHAKESPEARE AND *MUCH ADO ABOUT NOTHING*

When Shakespeare wrote *Much Ado About Nothing,* he was right in the middle of his career as a writer, actor and manager for a London theatre company, the Lord Chamberlain's Men. He had begun working with them when they formed in 1594, after moving to London from Stratford-upon-Avon. He stayed in London until around 1510.

Based on a bestseller

Shakespeare realized that people liked watching plays based on stories they already knew. Many theatre-goers at the time would have been familiar with Italian writers like Ariosto and their books, meaning they would have enjoyed the play even more. The same thing happens today, when bestselling books are turned into blockbuster movies.

Drawing crowds

During this time, Shakespeare wrote a variety of different types of play – gory, murderous tragedies, history plays about real-life people from the past, and lighter romances and comedies. His company needed a steady supply of plays of all kinds to attract paying audiences, and to impress the royal family, who they sometimes performed for too.

Much Ado is the work of an experienced writer who knew what his audiences wanted – moving love stories, comedy characters like Dogberry the police chief, and an evil villain to boo. With Beatrice and Benedick's wisecracking wit, the play also took quick-fire, sophisticated dialogue to a new level. It had something for everyone.

STAGING *MUCH ADO ABOUT NOTHING*

In Shakespeare's time, most people didn't read *Much Ado* as a book – they went to see it at the theatre. What were performances like in those days?

London theatres

Shakespeare's theatre company, the Lord Chamberlain's Men, put on their plays in various places – at royal palaces, law schools, pub courtyards, and in specially built open-air theatres such as The Theatre and the Curtain. In 1599, soon after *Much Ado* was written, they even built their own theatre, the Globe, on the south bank of the River Thames.

The Globe theatre

A trip to the Globe

The Globe theatre was ring-shaped, with three storeys of seating covered by a roof, and a standing area around the stage in the middle. Plays were mostly shown in the afternoon to make use of daylight, and were informal, noisy occasions. People wandered in and out, chatted, ate snacks and even shouted and threw things at the actors!

The actors wore costumes and used props, but there wasn't much scenery, as the company switched between different plays all the time. There were no women actors – younger men or boys with high voices played female roles. Lead roles went to the company's star actor, Richard Burbage, while the clown and dancer Will Kempe played comic roles, such as Dogberry in *Much Ado*.

Modern Globe

Today, you can see Shakespeare's plays at a modern replica of the Globe theatre, near its original site in London.

Was *Much Ado* a hit?

There are no records of exactly when *Much Ado About Nothing* was first shown, or if it was performed at the Globe. The first performance on record was at a royal palace in 1612 or 1613, to celebrate the wedding of Princess Elizabeth, King James I's daughter.

However, *Much Ado* was first printed in book form as early as 1600, and the title page said the Lord Chamberlain's Men had already performed it many times. This suggested it had been shown at the Globe, and was a big hit.

MUCH ADO ABOUT NOTHING THEMES AND SYMBOLS

In many of Shakespeare's plays, there are repeated themes and images that reinforce the play's main ideas. Here are some of the key themes in *Much Ado About Nothing*:

Disguise and deception

The image of hiding behind a disguise or appearing to be someone else crops up repeatedly.

*Leonato throws a fancy-dress party with masks as disguises.

*When Benedick wears his mask, Beatrice pretends not to know who he is.

*When Margaret meets Borachio, she appears to the onlookers to be Hero, as that is who they expect to see.

*The ultimate surprise disguise is used in the final scene, when Claudio thinks he is marrying a stranger – who turns out to be Hero, his lost love.

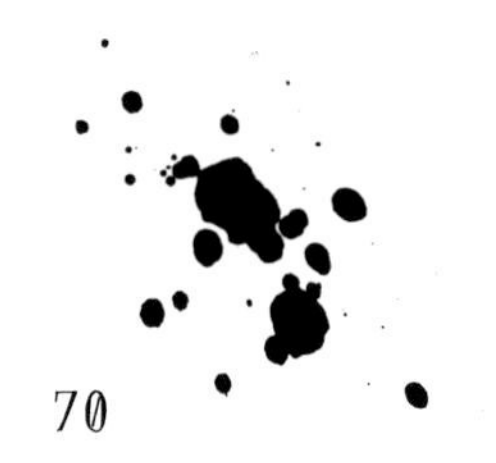

Etiquette and courtly behaviour

As soldiers, Don Pedro and his men are expected to follow the medieval tradition of courtly, or polite, behaviour.

For example, Benedick is not openly rude to Beatrice – he dresses up his insults in witty chit-chat. Claudio lets the more experienced Don Pedro court Hero for him, to hide his nerves. And Benedick cannot think of simply killing Claudio, which would be dishonourable. But he can challenge him to a duel – the gentleman's method of resolving disagreements. Even Don John remains polite throughout, while scheming behind everyone's backs.

Yet Shakespeare is actually interested in the strong feelings that lie behind all this role-playing – the passion, anxiety, jealousy and loneliness in his characters' hearts. He contrasts the brave faces people put on against the true feelings that actually control their behaviour.

Women

The play explores some of the views of women that were around in Shakespeare's time – that they were flighty, likely to be unfaithful, and all the same. Claudio and Don Pedro easily accept that Hero is a cheat, despite her previous good character. Claudio readily accepts the idea of marrying a completely different woman in her place. Benedick fears that a wife would just henpeck him or cheat on him.

Yet the women in the play actually contradict all these messages. Beatrice is Benedick's equal in wit and brains. Hero is actually far more loyal to Claudio than he is to her. Again, Shakespeare shows how reality does not always match the stories everyone tells each other.

MUCH ADO ABOUT "NOTING"

In Shakespeare's time, the title "*Much Ado about Nothing*" worked as a pun. "Nothing" was pronounced in a similar way to another word, "noting", which meant noticing, observing and watching people, or spreading rumours and gossip. It also meant writing notes and messages.

All about noting

If you look at *Much Ado* in this way, it's clear that almost all the action happens because of "noting".

• Hero is wrongly accused because of what Claudio and Don Pedro observe when they watch her window from a distance – and thanks to Don John's rumour-spreading.

• It is the Friar's careful "noting" of the true feelings on Hero's face that saves her – and Claudio's written words on her grave that make amends to her.

• Dogberry is so inefficient and long-winded, he can only finally get his vital message through to Leonato when he goes to the town clerk to have it noted down.

• Beatrice and Benedick only fall in love because their friends take note of how they really feel, and set up fake conversations for them to "secretly" note, or eavesdrop on. Their love notes come into play at the end as the final evidence of their love.

Noting and society

Why did Shakespeare make so much of this idea in *Much Ado*? He knew that the relationships that make up society are not just based on what people say about themselves, but about what people notice, think and say about each other. This "noting" can make or ruin someone's life – in the play, Hero loses, and then regains, everything because of it.

It's no different today, even though we use other methods, like social networks and forums, to spread these messages, observations and rumours. In fact, thanks to the Internet, the importance of "noting" may now be even greater.

Fun Fact!

Balthasar, Leonato's musician, also makes a pun on the word "noting" before he sings his song in the orchard. He uses it to mean his musical notes, which he jokes are not worth "noting", or bothering with.

Note this before my notes:
There's not a note of mine that's worth the noting.

THE LANGUAGE OF *MUCH ADO ABOUT NOTHING*

As well as being a playwright, Shakespeare was a poet, and often used very poetic language in his plays. In fact, most of them are mainly written in a type of verse, called blank verse. However, *Much Ado About Nothing* is unusual – it's mainly written in prose, or normal speech.

Poetic moments

However, some parts of the play are written in blank verse. Here is an example from the sad scene where Claudio and Don Pedro have visited what they believe to be Hero's grave. The regular rhythm of the lines makes them sound grand and serious, and they are filled with striking images.

Don Pedro:

Good morrow, masters,** put your torches out.

The wolves have prey'd, and look, the gentle day**

Before the wheels of Phoebus* round about

Dapples** the drowsy** east with spots of grey.**

Thanks to you all, and leave us. Fare you well.

Claudio:

Good morrow, masters.** Each his several way.**

Each line has five slow beats, or stresses.

* This metaphor describes the sun as the chariot of Phoebus, the ancient Greek sun god.

** Shakespeare uses rhyme, repetition and alliteration – pairs or groups of words that start with the same sound – to set up gentle, echoing patterns.

Quick-fire dialogue

The prose in *Much Ado* suits the types of conversations the characters have – a lot of witty, banter-filled chit-chat between friends. The informal, everyday speech patterns make Beatrice and Benedick's arguments and emotional moments feel more realistic and modern than Shakespeare's usual style. Here is an example from the end of the play:

BENEDICK: Come, I will have thee. But by this light, I take thee for pity.

BEATRICE: I would not deny you. But by this good day, I yield upon great persuasion, and partly to save your life, for I was told you were in a consumption.

BENEDICK: Peace, I will stop your mouth. [kissing her]

DON PEDRO: How dost thou, Benedick, the married man?

Did you know?

Shakespeare was the first to write down many of the words and phrases we still use today. In *Much Ado*, they include:

lie low   employer   schoolboy   reclusive

WHAT *MUCH ADO ABOUT NOTHING* MEANS TODAY

Why do we still enjoy Shakespeare's works today, more than 400 years after they were written? One reason is that Shakespeare was brilliant at choosing topics that everyone can relate to, whoever they are, and whenever in history they live. There are several great examples of this in *Much Ado About Nothing*:

Love-hate relationships

It's still common for people to start off not liking each other, then fall in love – or for their friends to set them up, as happens to Beatrice and Benedick in the play. In fact, ideas like these are still used in romcom movies. It makes a great ending when the warring couple finally admit their love.

Words, wit and manners

Much Ado explores the way people use witty banter and the rules of polite behaviour to put up a false "front". This is part of human nature, and something we all still do. People may do it to hide their true feelings and intentions, like Don John in the play. Or they may do it to avoid looking foolish, or to try to make people like them.

Who cheated on whom?!

Since ancient times, humans have been fascinated by gossip and scandalous stories about each other, and today's gossip magazines show we still are. *Much Ado* looks at how easily everyone is taken in by a false rumour, and the damage it can do.

Modern versions

Like many popular Shakespeare plays, *Much Ado* isn't just performed on stage in its original form – it's been made into several films too, often with big stars in the leading roles. There's also a spin-off opera called *Beatrice et Benedict*, a Bollywood film version, *Dil Chahta Hai*, and even musical and rock-opera versions.

GLOSSARY

alliteration	Grouping together words with the same initial letter
blank verse	A type of non-rhyming poetry used by Shakespeare
courtly	Polite; behaving according to traditional rules
dialogue	Conversation between characters
dramatis personae	A list of characters in a play
ducat	A type of gold coin
herald	A declaration
jester	A clown, joker or comedy performer
metaphor	Describing something as another thing to compare them
playwright	An author of plays
prose	Text written in ordinary sentences, not in verse
stage directions	Instructions for the actors in a play
yield	To give in

GLOSSARY OF SHAKESPEARE'S LANGUAGE

adieu	goodbye
coil	a commotion, hustle and bustle
consumption	a disease that makes someone waste away
cross	to thwart, stop or annoy someone
dear	precious or valuable
doth	does
ere	before
heartburned	given indigestion, or left feeling annoyed
hither	here
morrow	morning
noting	noticing, taking note of, gossiping or writing down
o'er	over
pray	to beg or plead
prey'd	preyed, or hunted and eaten prey
several	different
start-up	upstart, or a young, ambitious person
tartly	scowling or bitter
thee	you
thy	your

MUCH ADO ABOUT NOTHING QUIZ

Test yourself and your friends on the story, characters and language of Shakespeare's *Much Ado About Nothing*. You can find the answers at the bottom of the page.

1) How is Beatrice related to Leonato?
2) How does Don Pedro plan to help Claudio win Hero's love?
3) Why does Don John hate Claudio?
4) What plant does Beatrice hide behind in the orchard?
5) What excuse does Benedick give for his change of mood?
6) What is the name of police chief Dogberry's deputy?
7) Which three people are sure Hero is innocent?
8) What does Beatrice want Benedick to do to show he loves her?
9) Whose daughter is Claudio told he must marry?
10) What happens to Don John at the end of the play?

1) She is his niece
2) By talking to her at the party to let her know Claudio loves her
3) Because he is jealous that Don Pedro prefers Claudio to him
4) Honeysuckle
5) Toothache
6) Verges
7) The Friar, Beatrice and Benedick
8) Kill Claudio
9) The daughter of Antonio, Leonato's brother
10) He is caught and put in prison

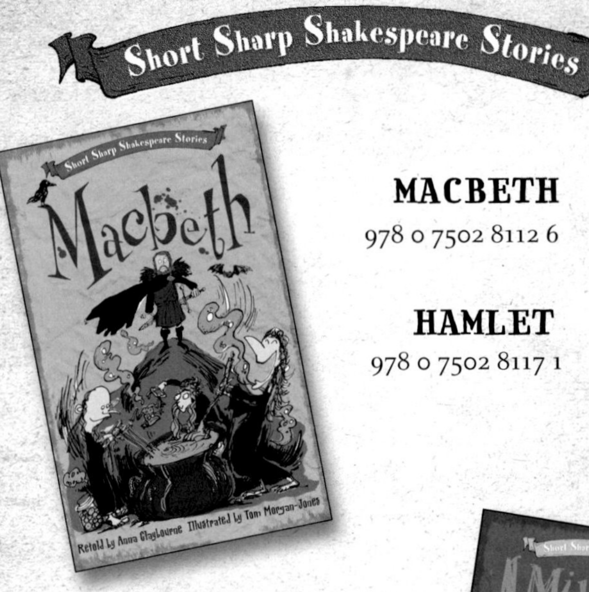

MACBETH

978 0 7502 8112 6

HAMLET

978 0 7502 8117 1

A MIDSUMMER NIGHT'S DREAM

978 0 7502 8113 3

THE TEMPEST

978 0 7502 8115 7

ROMEO AND JULIET

978 0 7502 8114 0

MUCH ADO ABOUT NOTHING

978 0 7502 8116 4